AMANDA AND RUTH ADVENTURES

TABLE OF CONTENTS

ACKNOWLEDGEMENT

I wish to thank our daughter, Taylor, for inspiring me to first tell her when she was 5 years old, the Amanda and Ruth Adventures and then encouraging me to write them.

As usual, my thanks to Doreen Strait, who does the computer work needed to turn this into a book.

A special thanks to granddaughter, Edy Maeve Wellington, eight, who illustrated this book with her imaginative drawings.

AMANDA AND RUTH ADVENTURES

BACKSTORY

The purposes of writing this Backstory are to enhance the reading pleasure of the reader; to enable me to write this book without constantly repeating details; and to provide me with additional stories to relate and write.

The cast of fiction characters are:

Amanda, five years old; 43 inches tall; weighs near 42 pounds; is slim and athletic; has reddish brown hair; green sparkling eyes; a somewhat crooked smile; her face is basically heart shaped and she has an outgoing personality and is the instigator of adventures but will also follow the lead of Ruth.

Amanda is the daughter of Rosalie and is the sole first cousin of Ruth. Amanda and Ruth were born on the same date so they have a shared birthday. Her dad, Ted, died in a private plane crash about two years prior. Amanda has no financial problems and does have a substantial trust fund. Although she has a profound bond with Ruth they have been together not very often since she moved with her parents from Los Angeles, California when she was only 9 months old.

Ruth, five years old, is one inch shorter than Amanda at 42 inches; weighs about 45 pounds; has jet black shiny hair; has light blue eyes which often light up; and has a somewhat husky build. Her face is round and she has a wide smile; she has an extrovert personality and sometimes is the starter of adventures.

Ruth is the daughter of Anita and has lived in Los Angeles all her life till the move to New York City when 5. She is not wealthy. Her father, Richard, left about two days after the death of Ted in the plane crash. Ruth believes her father will return.

Rosalie, 32 years old, is the older by one year of Anita, her sister; is five foot seven inches tall; weighs near 130; has blond hair; and dark blue eyes. She is an editor for a major publishing house in New York City and works from her apartment she owns in upper 83rd Street in New York; earns a good salary; has several authors she works with; and is considered beautiful. Rosalie inherited a substantial amount due to death of her husband, Ted; and from insurance, so that she has zero financial issues.

Rosalie is an extrovert, has computer skills; and has been dating Dave for about 9 months. She feels good about Dave and the fact that Amanda and Dave have a good relationship.

Ted told her some mysterious facts about his life that occurred before he and Rosalie met. Before taking the fatal flight, Ted told Rosalie that this related to his premarital life and it was necessary for the benefit of the United States.

Rosalie and Amanda missed Ted and grieved for him but have gone on with their lives.

Anita, 31 years old; is five foot five inches tall; and usually weighs 125 pounds; is athletic and runs and works out; her hair is brown with streaks; her eyes are a hazel shade; she has always been optimistic; her career is teaching special needs or exceptional children particularly children with autism. When she came to New York her first goal was to volunteer with the NYC public school system to help autistic children and she spent three days a week doing so. She loved Richard, her husband but he was reluctant and would not disclose his past.

A while before his sudden disappearance, he told Anita that he was in danger and feared for his life and the lives of Anita and Ruth and will have to vanish. Richard briefly alluded to a mission for the United States where he, Ted the husband of Rosalie, Max the cabbie, and someone named Dave, successfully prevented along with others, a real terror threat to this country. He also said that a terrorist group from that mission had targeted all who were on the mission for death but measures were in place to warn them if an attack was imminent.

Two days after Ted died in the plane crash, Richard received a call at two in the morning. He kissed and hugged Anita and told her to have faith that he would return. Before leaving he went into Ruth's bedroom and gently kissed Ruth and whispered "Believe-I will return". For the last two years nothing has been heard from Richard.

Anita, for many reasons and in part loneliness and a desire for her and Ruth to be part of the family life of Rosalie and Amanda asked her sister to come to live in New York. Rosalie said "sure".

Max, the self-employed Cabbie, 46 years old, a widower, and childless, had curly, blondish hair; golden eyes; is over six foot tall; weighs 180 pounds; is very strong; is a good boxer and a very good martial arts and karate expert. His face is square and he has a strong jaw. He has a controlled temper.

He was on several missions with Ted and Richard and sometime with Dave, the now boyfriend of Rosalie. He does not talk about that time of his life. Long ago, he made a pledge to both Ted and Richard that he would protect with his life and skills, Amanda and Rosalie and if they ever needed him, Ruth and Anita. As soon as Ted and Rosalie married followed a little over a year later by the birth of Amanda, Max has been on call as a Cabbie and has fulfilled his pledge as protector. Max invented and created a video game and sold it, for a fortune. He does not need his cab to make a living. He still works on video games and his quietly written but not published two books. One book, a non-fiction regarding his secret life on missions and the other regarding his secret passion of poetry. Max is basically a kind person but he is when needed very dangerous.

Dave, 35 years old, is five foot ten inches tall; weighs 175 pounds; has unruly dark brown hair; and brown eyes. Dave is an attorney and often works pro bono in clinics. He has never married and has no children. He played a supervisory role in the few missions that Ted, Richard, and Max conducted with others but did get to know them and admired them.

Dave met Rosalie about a year after Ted died when Rosalie and an author she was the editor for, George, came to the pro bono legal clinic. Rosalie and George came there to see if the clinic would allow George to research a fiction book he was writing about a lawyer who spent time in a legal clinic. Rosalie met Dave and he agreed to spend time with George on that research project. Rosalie on some occasions in her capacity of Editor would see Dave with George.

Dave finally asked Rosalie to go to dinner and she agreed. During the next nine months, Dave having completed his visits with George, dated Rosalie exclusively. Dave had met Amanda and they got along well. Dave also became well acquainted with Anita and Ruth. Dave revealed to Rosalie and Anita his more than casual relationship with Ted, Richard and Max. Dave also renewed his friendship with Max.

Ted died at age 33 in the plane crash. Ted was an investment banker and had through wise investments, became financially secure. He had wisely set up a trust fund for Rosalie and Amanda and added to it over the years so upon his death it was substantial. Ted also had inheritances from his deceased parents and from both an uncle and an aunt. This enabled him to buy with no debt the valuable and comfortable apartment. Ted left Rosalie and Amanda well off.

Richard, was 34 years old when he vanished for the last two years, was a major player in the movie industry and had earned a large salary. Richard was six foot tall; weighed 185 pounds; had graying hair and piercing blue eyes; was handsome and fit. Richard was debonair; was usually courteous; and did have deep love for Anita and Ruth, and they reciprocated. It never even entered the mind of Anita to contemplate a divorce. She firmly believed as did Ruth that Richard would someday walk in the door wherever they lived.

AMANDA AND RUTH ADVENTURES

CHAPTER ONE - REVELATIONS

On a bright sunny evening, Ruth and Anita flew from Los Angeles to New York City and after an uneventful flight landed at JFK airport. They were met at the baggage area by Amanda, Rosalie, and Max. After hugs and kisses, four large suitcases were in their possession and they all went out to the cab owned by Max.

Both Anita and Ruth were jet lagged and after eating a simple meal they went to sleep.

The next day Amanda was acquainting Ruth with the elevators, the building, and generally both girls were getting to know each other. Ruth told Amanda that it would be a good idea if she had her first slumber party and would come to the bedroom of Amanda and they would frankly discuss many matters. In particular they would talk about Ted, dad of Amanda, and Richard, father of Ruth.

During the day Anita and Rosalie discussed many matters. Rosalie told Anita that it was great for Amanda to have her only first cousin, Ruth, here and they surely will bond as Anita and Rosalie did until their marriages which happened within a three month span but they remained in contact. Over the years there had been visits so all could be together. They spent some time recalling matters re: Ted and Richard. Rosalie said that the heavy grieving time had lasted a year or so and that Ted was sorely missed by herself and Amanda.

Anita brought up the subject of Max and they both were aware of the bond between Max and Ted and Richard. They knew that Max would always be their protector.

CHAPTER ONE - REVELATIONS

Anita asked about Dave and Rosalie responded that they have been dating for nine months exclusively. Rosalie mentioned that Dave would be over for supper on Thursday.

Anita said she had sold her vehicle and almost all the furniture. Anita was fortunate that she and Richard had rented the house in Los Angeles and had not bought a home. She also said that almost all of the clothes and belongs of Richard had been donated. Anita also said Ruth had sorted out her clothes and toys and had donated many to the Salvation Army.

Rosalie asked Anita about her career and Anita said she was going to work about six hours a day three days a week at NYC Autism Center Public School and she had to finalize this in a day or two. A moving van would arrive in a week so that Anita and Ruth would have their additional personal belongings.

Rosalie told Anita that she and Ruth were more than welcome and she did not want to have any thought by Anita of paying Rosalie any rent, etc.

They did recall their childhood together with fondness. Rosalie also said she has a cleaning service on call and also has a tutoring service which is available now for Ruth depending on What Ruth either needs or desires. Anita and Rosalie retired to their rooms.

About an hour before they were to go to sleep, Ruth came to the bedroom of Amanda and again expressed her elation on being in NYC and the opportunity to bond with Amanda; to be with Max more often; and her wish to meet Dave.

CHAPTER ONE - REVELATIONS

They both donned pajamas and curled up in bed. Amanda said she would talk to Ruth about her dad, Ted, and then Ruth would tell about Richard, her father.

Amanda said she and her Mom had grieved and cried about her dad for about a year but now had fully accepted his death. Amanda showed Ruth the album with pictures of her dad, Ted and pointed out several photos where Ted and Richard were portrayed.

Amanda related many memories she had of her dad and what he told her. She said he always tucked her in bed and kissed her and said "I love you and always will, Amanda." He never forgot to ask about her and what she learned and did. Amanda made it clear that she missed her dad and would never forget him. Amanda also volunteered that she is growing to love Dave not as a substitute replacement dad but for what he had brought to Rosalie, a true caring for her, and she had the hope and wish that Dave and Rosalie would marry sometime. She mentioned that her dad and Ruth's father, Richard, and Max had been on "missions" in the past and strangely enough that Dave was in some way involved.

Ruth gave Amanda a fierce hug and told her she felt the sorrow and pain of "Amanda.

Ruth said "Amanda, I am thinking that you and I are going to have great adventures together and we will take turns in being the instigator". Amanda said this was a great idea and she was all for it.

Ruth then with a halting voice lovingly told Amanda about her father, Richard. Her father also tucked her in bed at night, hugged and kissed her and very often told her a new made-

CHAPTER ONE - REVELATIONS

up story each night. Ruth said she had in the last few months started to write down these tales.

Her father had to vanish until he had completed his mission or died trying to remove the threat to himself, Ruth and Anita.

She and Anita have kept the faith and truly believe that her father will come back someday. Ruth stated that she misses her father and wished with all of her mind, heart, and being that he was safe and healthy and would succeed.

Amanda took Ruth in an embrace and told Ruth that she also believed that Richard would return.

Reiterating that tomorrow they would go with Max to the Zoo and have their first adventure, Amanda and Ruth holding hands fell asleep.

by
Edy

CHAPTER TWO - ZOO NOMAD

One day Ruth asked Amanda when they would go to the New York Zoo and Amanda said, "We will go today." Amanda called to make sure that Max had his cab available to take them to the zoo. It was and they went. At the zoo they visited the elephant area and they admired the size of the elephants and their tusks. There were at least a dozen elephants roaming around with three young ones capering. Ruth asked "Why could they not adopt one of the baby elephants" but Amanda opined that the bathtub would not be large enough to give the baby elephant a bath and otherwise the odor would be too much for their mothers. "You know how fragile (a new word for Amanda) Anita's nose is", Ruth agreed. They later visited the enclosure holding "zillion" monkeys of all shapes and hues. Ruth particularly liked a small monkey with a bright red tail who was engaged in antics which annoyed the older monkeys and at least two older monkeys chased the little monkey which Ruth named "Nomad".

Ruth told Amanda that they should rescue Nomad and she pointed out that any of the bathtubs would be large enough to give "Nomad" a bath when needed. Amanda noticed two small doors at the side and one of them was propped open by a barrier. Ruth went through the open door while Amanda stood guard. Ruth had a good sized tote bag with her. It was somewhat humorous to see Ruth toting the bag and silently creeping amidst the monkeys. She walked somewhat like the monkeys walked and kept her arms hanging loose. Ruth did not try to chatter like the monkeys did but kept grimacing and baring her teeth. One large monkey saw Ruth and came over and wrapped his arms around her, squeezing her and Ruth just patted this monkey on his head and tweaked his nose, causing the monkey to let Ruth go. Ruth reached "Nomad" and she coaxed him to go in the tote bag. Ruth had some trouble

CHAPTER TWO - ZOO NOMAD

dragging the bag back to the open door but finally managed to do so. Both girls took one of the bag handles and carried the tote bag with "Nomad" in it to the cab. Max asked them why the bag was so heavy and Amanda told Max that "No" was in it making up a nickname on the spot for "Nomad".

They arrived back at the apartment and told Rosalie they had to give "Nomad" a bath. For some strange reason Rosalie did not bother to ask what or who was " Nomad" or why a bath was needed although it was very noticeable that Ruth specifically had dirty hands and knees and that even Amanda who usually had a "clean fetish" appeared to need a bath also.

Instead of the bathtub, Amanda and Ruth used the large sink to give Nomad a "bath" by filling it with warm soapy water, using the lavender soap lotion. They used a bench so they could work as a bath team and both of them washed and scrubbed "Nomad". They took him out to show and tell Anita and Rosalie. Anita told them they would at once take Nomad back to the zoo so he could rejoin his family. They did so without difficulty, thereby ending their first zoo adventure.

By
Edy

CHAPTER THREE - LOST IN LIBRARY

Amanda and Ruth were taken to the library by Rosalie and they went into the large children's rooms. There were a large number of children there some with an adult and some without. Rosalie told Amanda and Ruth they should stay there and read a book and also select one or more books to take home while she went to see someone about a fund-raising event for about thirty minutes. Soon after Rosalie left, Ruth said she needed to go to the bathroom and they asked where it was located and were told it was the second door on the right down the hallway. Both of them went and used the bathroom facilities and then Ruth saw another large door on the left with large bright brass knobs and a seal with the word ENTRE. Amanda read this and told Ruth this meant enter in English. They each turned the knobs and the door opened revealing a magnificent room filled with knight's armor; swords; spears; and military equipment. In exploring, Ruth found a small door on a wall and pulled it open. There before them was a wooden cage with pulleys. Ruth climbed in and Amanda followed. Amanda pushed a button and they started to go down for three stories till the dumbwaiter stopped and a door in that lower level wall opened automatically allowing both girls to exit. The door closed behind them and would not reopen despite their efforts. They knew they were stranded in the lower area of the library and that Rosalie would be looking for them. They were also sure that Max would join in the search.

Amanda succeeded in finding the light switch and they found themselves in a somewhat dusty round room with no windows and having boxes piled up all around. In searching for a way out they saw what appeared to be a metal door about eight feet higher up with a large ring on it. They moved some boxes and

CHAPTER THREE - LOST IN LIBRARY

piled them up so they could climb up and with some effort pulled on the ring opening the metal door. They saw a tunnel and observed a sliver of light far down the tunnel. They talked about their predicament and decided to crawl through the tunnel. They both could read and knew their vital statistics such as names, addresses, telephone numbers and Ruth even knew her own social security number although Amanda said that information was useless. Ruth countered with the concept that her social security number would help to prove her identity and then she could identify Amanda.

It seemed to take them a long time to reach the end of the tunnel and then they both worked to open from the inside the latches holding the gate closed. They prevailed and had to jump three feet down to the ground and did so by holding onto the gate and edge of the metal tunnel and were quite happy to be outside on the ground. They found themselves in a cemetery and decided to walk on a path northwardly and reached an open gate to a street. They had their purses with them and had some money but no cell phone. They located a store and used the pay phone and called Max on his cell phone. They had been missing for about one and half hours and their mothers, Rosalie and Anita, Max and the library personnel were frantic. Within ten minutes Max in his cab with the mothers arrived and all was well. In searching the library no one looked in the military room that the girls had entered since in trying that door it was locked and could not be opened. It was later determined that by opening and entering the dumbwaiter device that the hallway door locked itself for safety reasons. Also no one had used that tunnel for over ten years and hardly anyone in the library system even remembered it existed.

CHAPTER THREE - LOST IN LIBRARY

Both Ruth and Amanda said they wanted to return to the library since they had not had a chance to select and check out books to read. They did return and each selected a mystery novel to read and both books involved caves or other hiding places so that both Ruth and Amanda felt at home with their books, having had their library adventure.

CHAPTER FOUR - MAX AND THE MEDALLION

On a sultry Saturday morning when the forecast was light rain, after they ate breakfast, Ruth asked Amanda if she wanted to visit with Max and make arrangements with him to take them for a cab ride later in the morning. They went to the cab stand and discovered that Max was not there and in talking to Pete, another friendly cabbie, they learned that in fact, Max had not been in his usual spot for the last two days. They went to their apartment and asked Anita to call Max. After three rings, Max answered his cell phone and after some delay told Anita that the Taxicab Commission was holding his Medallion. His medallion is his cab license and without a Medallion, he cannot drive his cab but he said he could not talk about it on the phone. Anita was quite disturbed since Max spent one year acquiring the Medallion. Anita told Max to get a cab and some to the apartment. After protesting, Max complied and arrived about forty minutes later.

Max came into the living room and Anita, Rosalie, Amanda and Ruth were eagerly waiting for him. After much urging, Max told them that allegations were made that he was overcharging by rigging the meter and that he did not turn in a woman's purse. Pending a complete investigation, Max's Medallion would be held in escrow. Max thought it might be six months before the matter would be resolved and he believed that he could lose. He had taken the cab to a new repair shop a few days before and his meter did not look the same after that. He stated that he had found the purse and as is customary turned it in at the "lost and found" office of the cab company but since he had a fare waiting did not get a receipt for the lost purse. Later, Amanda went to Ruth's bedroom and told Ruth that they should go to the lost and found office and she showed Ruth two mini-cassette

CHAPTER FOUR - MAX AND THE MEDALLION

devices that her mother had spent a little time showing Ruth how to operate the devices. They took a cab with Pete driving and asked Pete to wait for them. They talked to the clerk, after turning on the recorders so that each would have a record. The clerk, Roger, was on the phone and could not see the girls since their heads just reached the top of the counter and they both recorded his conversation where he was saying that if he got enough cabbies in trouble that his two nephews would be able to buy the forfeited Medallions thereby realizing their dreams to be cabbies. He mentioned Max by name as one he had targeted both by keeping the returned purse and he also had steered Max to the unscrupulous repair shop which was where he had sent other cabbies that likewise were in trouble for fraudulent matters. Ruth got the attention of the clerk and while she kept him occupied, Amanda went behind the counter and after some effort found a hidden drawer with many items including the purse that Max was accused of stealing.

In the meanwhile, Rosalie and Anita hired a private detective and the two person detective team was in the living room when Amanda and Ruth returned. They took turns telling about their adventure and had everyone listen to the cassettes. The detectives wrote up a report and had Amanda and Ruth read and then sign it. They went to the repair shop with police officers and an arrest occurred when it was discovered the fraud schemes of rigging meters and they found meters that were being rigged. A confession was obtained implicating the clerk, Roger. They then went to the lost and found department confronting Roger and locating all the stolen items. Roger confessed about his scheme and Max was immediately exonerated.

CHAPTER FOUR - MAX AND THE MEDALLION

On Sunday, Max, in his cab with his Medallion restored, took Ruth and Amanda on a cab trip into and around Central Park. Ruth and Amanda had earned their newest nicknames "The Little Bright Detectives".

CHAPTER FIVE - LETTERS

During the day, Amanda asked Ruth whether they should share the last letters that they had from their fathers. They brought their treasure boxes to Ruth's room and silently opened them. Ruth told Amanda, "You go first since you are the host cousin".

Amanda pulled out an envelope and unfolded the letter. She read:

To my lovely daughter, Amanda.

I am flying a plane this evening. I am on a mission for our nation. I expect to be back in three days. I want so badly to tuck you in and kiss your lovely face. I love you more than life itself.

I know you will grow up to be as beautiful as your mom and you will have a wonderful life.

I will always hold you and Rosalie in my heart. Be good and kind and always use your mind.

Amanda spoke with tears in her eyes "It ends with "eternal love—your Dad."

Ruth grabbed hold of Amanda and saying nothing, her long intense hug saying what words could not.

Ruth carefully handled her letter from her father and in a halting voice started to read:

To Little "R" my one and only daughter, Ruth.

You remember that I once told you about another Ruth who was strong, faithful and always loyal. Please be brave and give your mother, my beloved, Anita, hugs and kisses from me. I have kissed you for the last time until I come back home. There is danger and evil in the world. I am leaving to keep all of us safe. I am not free to say more.

CHAPTER FIVE - LETTERS

Be happy. Enjoy every moment of your existence. I repeat that when the danger is past, I will come home. Remember me in your dreams and heart. Believe.

Ruth then ended with the words written by her father, Richard, "Always Love - Big "R" (father)".

Amanda held Ruth close for what seemed forever. Amanda and Ruth very carefully returned their letters to their treasure boxes.

They knew in their hearts that they had an unshakeable bond between them.

CHAPTER SIX - PARTY MIXUP MISCHIEF?

Rosalie planned a bridal shower for her friend, Trish, for a Sunday afternoon and by coincidence or design Anita planned to have a baby shower for Rita on the same Sunday at the same time, both at the apartment. It took some time for each to learn of the other's plan it being revealed when Joan, a friend of both Anita and Rosalie received two invitations and specifically since she was the aunt of the mother-to-be, Rita. Anita and Rosalie met and discussed this matter and agreed to continue to hold the two showers using the living room for one and the recreation room for the other. It was decided that no children would be present and this included the absence of Amanda and Ruth. However, men could attend either or both of the showers. Amanda was quite disturbed that she was not permitted to attend these parties since she did attend similar parties previously and she decided to get even for this slight.

Most of the presents were delivered by the Saturday before the showers and they were placed on tables in each of the party rooms.

Amanda very early on Sunday morning moved presents around so they were all mixed up and then deliberately but carefully removed the cards or tags from many of them and placed them methodically on other presents.

At noon hour, Amanda and Ruth accompanied by their part-time nanny (babysitter according to the girls) went off to see a movie either Toy Story 3 or one of the Shrek ones and were to get a late lunch or early dinner and told not to return to the apartment until 6:00 p.m or later. The showers were due to start at two p.m. and Aunt Joan had asked to come early by one p.m. to assist in whatever needed still to be done. Joan after

CHAPTER SIX - PARTY MIXUP MISCHIEF?

helping out wanted to see her presents since she planned to attend in some fashion both showers. She found the present for Trish but immediately knew there was something wrong since the size of the box did not remotely match what she had purchased; similarly when she looked at the tag on her present for Rita was an odd shape and color and Joan knew some horrible error had occurred. As each guest arrived, and there were about sixty total, they were asked to see if their presents were as they had bought and delivered them. It turned out that most said mistakes occurred.

Anita and Rosalie were embarrassed but Rosalie said why don't we combine the showers by parting the doors between the rooms and when it came time to unwrap the presents that Trish and Rita would take turns an each of the guests would make sure which present was for which recipient. Anita said she would use the voice recognition program on the computer to record all data so that there would be a complete printout for all concerned.

The dual showers went forward without a hitch and everyone expressed sincere admiration that Rosalie and Anita had come up with such a clever plan and everyone had an enjoyable time. Rita and Trish had complete records of every gift and the donor making it very easy to prepare and send thank you notes.

In the meanwhile, Amanda could not keep a secret and she revealed to Ruth what she had done and why. Ruth had some sympathy for Amanda but thought that Amanda was going to be in serious trouble and she told Amanda that she would share the blame. However, Amanda said she would confess when they got home and take the punishment.

After a good meal, (Ruth thinking it may be the last good meal for Amanda) they returned home and Amanda promptly told the mothers what she had done. Strangely, neither Anita nor Rosalie were noticeably angry but Rosalie did tell Amanda, she could go on no more outings for one week and had to write a 50-word sincere apology to Anita, Rosalie, Trish and Rita. Amanda said why did she have to apologize to their nanny Rita and then was surprised to learn that the baby shower was for a different Rita. Amanda quietly accepted the punishment. Ruth later overheard Anita and Rosalie talking and heard them say how pleased they were at the dual showers and that Amanda caused this pleasurable event to occur. Wisely, Ruth kept this matter a secret from Amanda.

CHAPTER SEVEN - CAKE BAKE

Amanda told Ruth that her mother, Rosalie, had been so good lately that she would bake a cake for her mother. Ruth asked if she could help and was told by Amanda that her job would be to keep Rosalie busy and then Ruth could come into the kitchen to help out. Ruth decided she would ask Rosalie while her mother Anita was out to help Ruth with a dress that needed lengthening and Ruth got out her short red party dress and went off to see Rosalie in her bedroom. Rosalie liked to sew and design clothes so this was a perfect idea.

No one else was at home so Amanda went to the kitchen following directions to preheat the oven to 350 degrees in accord with directions for an "easy company" cake and Amanda had reread the recipe until she knew it by heart. She still kept the directions available since she wanted this baked cake to be very good. Amanda had to figure out the measurements were to use a 1/4 cup of butter; 1/2 cup of milk; 2 eggs; 1/3 cup of sugar; 3/4 cup of flour; 1 teaspoon of baking powder; 1/2 teaspoon of salt; also 1/4 teaspoon of almond extract-Amanda could not find this ingredient so she substituted 1/4 teaspoon of nutmeg and 1/4 teaspoon of cloves combining those together. She was very precise in following the instructions by melting the butter; stirring in milk and the combined nutmeg/cloves mixture; then adding sugar, salt, baking powder, egg mixture, and flour. Next, she added the butter and had a suitable pan available to put the batter in. Amanda then put this pan in the pre-heated oven and baked it for 25-30 minutes till done. Ruth had returned briefly and since Amanda did not have a frosting for the cake Ruth suggested using Nestles chocolate syrup and Amanda followed through covering the cake from the top and allowing the syrup to spread over the sides of the cake. In order to make

CHAPTER SEVEN - CAKE BAKE

the frosting more solid Amanda placed the cake in the freezer and promptly forgot that the cake was there for over two hours.

When Ruth asked her where the cake was Amanda went and got the cake out of the freezer and it was rock hard so Amanda decided to put the cake in the microwave to defrost it. She only left the cake in the microwave oven for two minutes at a time and after eight minutes, it was defrosted so that the syrup had re-melted and was gooey.

Amanda proudly took the cake in to where Rosalie was in the recreation room and also provided paper plates, napkins and spoons/forks. Rosalie, Anita, and Ruth bravely tasted Amanda's cake and all agreed it was certainly different and all wondered at the unusual taste while making a concerted effort to lick the delicious frosting off the cake. Part of the cake was mushy and a small part was icicle hard making it a treat to remember.

The kitchen was a disaster and took over 2 hours to clean.

BY
Edy

CHAPTER EIGHT - PUBLIC SCHOOLS

During the time that Ruth was with Amanda and their ongoing adventures, a serious matter had arisen. Both Anita and Rosalie believed that the public school system was inferior to and far less safe than private academies.

Soon after Anita and Ruth came to live with Rosalie and Amanda, they were preliminarily enrolled in Shadyside Academy. Despite that both Ruth and Amanda tested superior in all academic subjects, Shadyside Academy insisted that they would based on their ages have to attend kindergarten and to make matters worse, they would be separated. The reason provided was that for Amanda and Ruth to become independent and so that their special bond could be severed they like twins had to have separate paths in education. The Academy did say that after the first year, everything would be re-evaluated.

Rosalie reluctantly accepted this due to her deep feelings about safety. Anita based on her belief that the bond should not be interfered with did not agree.

Amanda and Ruth objected to both the separation and treating them like babies. They refused to be in kindergarten.

Anita and Rosalie checked out other private academies and found out that most had similar policies. They checked out the charter schools and found out that they usually believed separating the girls was the right way and in some ways were more rigid about placement of children by age.

Anita and Rosalie decided to expand the use of the tutoring service to in effect "home school" Amanda and Ruth and they accepted this decision.

CHAPTER EIGHT - PUBLIC SCHOOLS

While having adventures, Ruth and Amanda met many children who attended public school and both felt comfortable with them.

One evening Ruth asked Amanda to go on a public school adventure. She said "We can sneak in the school and attend some classes and see for ourselves how safe the school is and whether we would like the teachers, school, and kids. They talked to Max who was receptive and knew they would be safe and by being together would receive a good education since they would still have as needed or desired the tutoring service.

The next day, accompanied by Max, they went to the public school. Max said they had just come to New York and he was their great uncle. The school principal, Alice, said she would welcome them and they could take a summer course to start at first grade level and would learn together. Max promised that he would bring in their birth certificates, etc. During this first day, Amanda and Ruth were given an academic test. Susan, the teacher testing them, was astounded at the test results. Amanda was at least at 4th grade level in mathematics and science. Ruth was at 5th grade in reading and her knowledge of history was off the chart since the test stopped at 6th grade levels. Susan said there would be further testing in the future.

For two days, Amanda and Ruth attended summer school and were free to attend many classes. They especially enjoyed the fifth grade history class. Ruth wowed the teacher, Rose and class of 4th graders with her knowledge of history of Greece and Rome and actually taught the teacher some facts she had not known.

Anita and Rosalie discovered this latest adventure and on the third day went to the school and had a meeting with the principal, Alice, Susan, the Testing teacher, Rose, the history teacher, Max with Amanda and Ruth waited in the hallway.

Max had been chastised by Rosalie but stood his ground saying he protected the girls and there was no danger. Both Ruth and Amanda explained in detail how much they enjoyed this public school, the teachers, and the kids they met and socialized with. It was true that Amanda and Ruth were far younger in age than most children there and were obviously smaller and far less strong but they fit in and were accepted.

After a lengthy meeting it was decided that Amanda and Ruth for one year could attend this public school; would be together; would be allowed to be in different classes than other first graders would attend so that Ruth and Amanda could for example be in third grade for Math; fifth grade for science; and attend several different classes for reading, history and geography. This would be an experiment for the benefit of the school, the teachers, and the students. It was believed that the other students would benefit the most by having such gifted friendly children there.

Amanda and Ruth were elated, max was vindicated, and Rosalie and Anita were happy to have this issue resolved.

Ruth and Amanda started to compile a list of future adventures relating to public school. They were also pre-planning the brunch party scheduled for two days before school began when they, their mothers, Max, and Dave would have a party.

CHAPTER NINE - TOYS GO

Amanda and Ruth were watching television early one morning when an advertisement came on asking for toys to be donated to a children's shelter and stated that children aged three to twelve were at the shelter and had no toys to speak of. They decided to look at their toys and determine which ones they would donate. They found that they had boxes of stored toys they were not playing with and they asked Anita to take them to the shelter and max was called to drive them to the location in the Bronx. There were six boxes of toys to be delivered there. The drive took about 45 minutes each way and both girls were excited to be part of this gift errand.

The building was an older mansion converted to a live-in shelter for parents and children who were abused or children waiting to be placed in a foster care home. Upon entering Amanda and Ruth were thrilled to be greeted by ten children ranging in age from three to twelve, both boys and girls, and all of them smiling. They all helped to carry the boxes in and using the large parlor carefully removed the toys from the boxes and displayed them so the children could look and admire them, before making their choices. A major item was a circus style railroad set with animals and a circus tent. This was considered too advanced for Ruth so she willingly donated this for the enjoyment of the children occupying this building and to remain there for the future use of any child coming to the home. There were eight dolls so that each of the girls had two dolls to own and play with. There was a microscope set and two erector sets and Lincoln logs and Lego that there were many building sets along with Star wars sets and Barbie's and Bratz set pieces. For the artistic or creative children there were bead making kits, paint by number sets, puzzles, and modeling

CHAPTER NINE - TOYS GO

clay in addition to play-doh containers. There also were two child computer set ups so that games could be played and writings accomplished. Amanda and Ruth spent several hours with the children enjoying the experience and the interaction with them. Amanda and Ruth decide to continue to collect toys to donate to this shelter for the indefinite future knowing that they were doing good and gaining self-esteem and a real measure of self-worth. Their mothers, Anita and Rosalie, were vocal in their heartfelt praise for Amanda and Ruth and expressed their praise for them and told them their true reward that they had shown their value as human beings with their feelings for others.

CHAPTER TEN - PLAYGROUND BULLIES

One of the main pleasures for Amanda and Ruth was visiting Central Park and the many children playgrounds located there. They liked going there with either or both of their mothers or with their part-time nanny, Rita.

They liked the slides, swings, play tunnels and climbing structures. Very special were the forts and castles that they played in and on. This was very peaceful and enjoyable till the bullies arrived in the form of two brothers and a girl cousin who were 7,8,9 years old and were big and seemed to be strong. These bullies, named Joe, Dave and Stella would go around the playground, pulling kids' hair, tripping kids, walking up the wrong way on sliding boards, yelling like banshees, and causing turmoil particularly for the smaller children. Ruth stood up to the girl Stella and was knocked down bruising her left knee due to that action. It got so bad that many of the care givers started to avoid this playground but Amanda and Ruth wanted to play there and they had many friends who played there also.

One day, Ruth took her mother's miniature camcorder installed a cassette and reviewed the instructions for its operation and did several practice runs using this device. She placed it in a carry on bag and put a hole in the end of the bag so the lens could project out and set up a method to use her hand to operate this camcorder.

Ruth went to the playground and moved around filming the actions of the three bullies. The camcorder also had the ability which Ruth used to record sound so she was able to capture the voices, remarks, and even profanity being used by Joe, Dave and especially Stella. Ruth took the hour and a half

CHAPTER TEN - PLAYGROUND BULLIES

of video and audio back to the apartment and had Rosalie, Anita and Rita view this display of bullying by those three children.

The next day, Anita made some telephone calls inviting other parents and caregivers including those involved with Dave, Stella and Joe along with personnel from the playground and after a cordial visit took all of them to the recreation room to view the camcorder recorded production. At first, those related to the bullies said their children could not be doing and saying those things but as the show went on, they were compelled to admit and decry the bullying tactics. Additional copies were made available so that the bullies' parents could go home and have this seen by the bullies themselves.

The bullies were barred from all of Central Park playgrounds for four months and were warned that any repeat of their actions or vocal matters would result in a lifetime ban. The parents of the bullies set up a fund so that there would be a permanent display at each of the playgrounds demonstrating visually that there would be zero tolerance for bullying at the playgrounds. Ruth received accolades from many people for the realism displayed in both the video and audio pertaining to the camcorder, and for taking such decisive action against the bullies.

CHAPTER ELEVEN - HAIR AND LISP

One morning, while Rosalie was helping Amanda with her hair she said she thought something was seriously wrong because of all the snarls and entanglements in Amanda's hair. Rosalie asked Anita about this matter since some years before Anita had taken hair dressing courses but Anita was equally baffled. They took Amanda to the pediatrician who gave Amanda a thorough examination and tested a few strands of hair. The doctor said that he could not find any medical cause for the hair problem and suggested that Amanda be seen by a hair specialist who usually only handled hair matters of pre-teens.

The appointment was scheduled to last several hours and both Rosalie and Anita decided to accompany Amanda. It was decided that Ruth would stay at the apartment with Rita. Ruth was sullen and angry at being left out but Anita knew that Ruth would be bored sitting at the hair dressing salon with nothing to do, so it was arranged that Liza, the almost six year old niece of Rita, would spend the day to play with Ruth. Ruth was not happy about this since she did not know Liza except that Ruth was aware that Liza talked funny with a pronounced lisp. Rita told Ruth that Liza had a problem with the alignment of her jaw and vocal cords causing Liza to lisp. Ruth was still out of sorts and with great sighs and rolling of her eyes and after much urging by her mother, Anita, agreed to play with Liza.

Amanda was disturbed to having her hair be the focus of so much attention but realized that it should be determined what the problem and more importantly what the solution would be so that her hair could be brushed and again be luxurious and able to be handled in an attractive manner and she recognized this was not the case at this time.

CHAPTER ELEVEN - HAIR AND LISP

Kurt, the owner of the hair salon greeted all of them and performed an extensive examination of Amanda's hair. He and his assistants went into detail, telling Amanda, Rosalie and Anita that they should no longer use harsh chemicals on the hair and to limit the number of washings. The advice was to use soapy water with a very mild conditioner and to brush the hair with a counter-clockwise circular motion. After a thorough cleansing of Amanda's hair, Kurt clipped some hair from the sides back and a little from the top. Kurt demonstrated the brushing technique and had both Rosalie and Anita practice this and then had Amanda try the brushing technique and after several attempts Amanda became used to this circular brushing motion.

Kurt also provided samples of the conditioner and sold them two style brushes and gave them detailed instructions and brochures. Kurt assured them if they would follow this program that the luster and texture of Amanda's hair would be back to what it had been several months in the past and that there should be no further difficulty.

In the meanwhile, Ruth acted in a surly manner toward Liza and was unwilling to play board games with Liza claiming that since Liza spoke with such a bad lisp that Ruth could not understand her and did not want to revert to sign language. Liza started to cry and told Ruth that she did not want to play with mean Ruth. Anita took both Ruth and Liza into the kitchen and made soup for them along with milk and a large oatmeal cookie. Rita told them a story of an orphan girl who suffered an injury at the time of the death of this girl's parents to that she could not hear not even the last words of the girls mothers which were "I Love You". As Rita told that tale she said that

CHAPTER ELEVEN - HAIR AND LISP

the little deaf girl went to college and became a leaned teacher
and most famously said that every person in the world has a
disability or infirmity and that what you do with your life is
always more important than whether you are hearing impaired, or
are blind or have speech difficulties. Rita pointed out that
Liza was trying to overcome her lisping and that Ruth was being
unfair to Liza and not giving her a chance caused by Ruth
feeling left out with regard to the hair problem of Amanda.
Rita also said that Ruth had wonderful hair and a very good
speaking voice and that Ruth's disability was her failure to cut
some slack with others and to be more forgiving. Rita asked
Ruth to go to her room for awhile and think about these matters.
Ruth did and came to the conclusion that she should be grateful
for all she has and to be more accepting of others. Ruth
returned and told Liza that she was truly sorry and promised to
mend her ways. Ruth and Liza played well together for the
remainder of the afternoon and when Amanda, Anita and Rosalie
returned they found Ruth and Liza engrossed in playing
Battleship game with Liza winning.

They stopped the game so they could look and touch Amanda's
beautiful new luxurious hairdo. Ruth asked if she could go to
this stylist and Liza chimed in also with her request. Without
pausing both Rosalie and Anita spoke together with a loud Yes
and Sure Why Not.

An appointment was made for the next Thursday and Amanda
was invited to go along.

This occurred and all three girls, Amanda, Ruth, and Liza
had a joint photo taken to demonstrate what wonderful hairdos
they had.

CHAPTER TWELVE - GROUND HOLE

Amanda and Ruth were in Max's cab driving to Central Park to watch ice skaters when they saw on a corner that a building was being demolished and there were trucks with men picking up debris. Max told them that this was going to be another high rise condo project but it would be fenced in for many months till all the permits were obtained. When they drove back later in the day, sure enough there was a high steel fence rising and heavy gates were ready to be installed. Ruth noticed and pointed out to Amanda that there was a small place in the fence where due to a depression in the earth, there was a small gap about a foot high. This construction site was just a block from Central Park. They went back to the park the next day and stayed at the garden and flower area and as soon as possible Ruth after encouraging Amanda to go with her made their way to the construction site and wiggled under the chain link fence. They went over to where there was a hole that slanted downward to where it appeared the old basement of the demolished building had been.

Ruth and Amanda walked and slid down the hole and Ruth took a flashlight from her back pack and gave Amanda a smaller flashlight. They wondered why this area was not filled in but realized that there were still a large area to search and there was a large amount of metal to be salvaged.

On one side of this vast expanse Ruth saw something protruding from what once was a wall. With the help of Amanda, Ruth priced a rectangular box about 12 inches long by 6 inches wide and 8 inches high. Strangely this silver colored heavy metal box was not locked but had a hinged side. Using both flashlights since this was a dark area of the basement, Ruth and

CHAPTER TWELVE - GROUND HOLE

Amanda carefully lifted the lid upward so they could see what the box contained.

There were four items that looked like medals such as athletes received and an inner container which was difficult to open. Ruth succeeded in opening it to reveal a good sized watch which was engraved on the back - To Eric from Jan-1940-SURE. The most unusual matter that the watch was still running and Ruth checked with her own watch that it was keeping accurately the time. There was also a card stating that Eric was placing his medals and watch in this box for safekeeping in 1942 since he was drafted and wanted them to go to Jan if anything happened to him.

Ruth and Amanda took the box with those items and struggled up the slanted dirt exit hole. They hurried back to the gardens at Central Park and told Rita who had been looking for them that they got interested in a certain flower display and did not realize how much time passed.

After they came home to their apartment, Amanda and Ruth borrowed Anita's computer and using her password which was "atina" proceeded to do research via the internet to see if they could discover anything about Eric, Jan, the medals, the watch or the building site. They did find out that the building was erected in 1934 and who the owners over the years were but had no success on the other matters.

They thought about these matters all evening and then decided they had better tell Anita and Rosalie about their deserted excavation site adventure. Rosalie, using her special magnifying glass, discovered a faint date on the card and more importantly saw and pointed out an address 2456 Elm Street, Erie, Pa. Rosalie went to the computer and using the high speed internet looked up the address and who was living there in the late 30's and early 40's. They found the names Eric Strauss and Jan Kimber who had lived on the first and second floor apartments at that time. Further research established that they, Erica and Jan had married in 1944 and had two children. The survivors in 2010 were several grandchildren since Jan and Eric had died in 1971 in a car crash and both of their children were also deceased. It was also determined that Eric won medals for swimming in high school. The watch itself was not valuable. The real mystery is why Eric never retrieved the box after returning from his wartime duties and why he hid the box in the first place in that building.

Anita through her contacts located the living grandchildren and invited the three of them to come to the apartment and the grandchildren, Alex, Bart, and Sally, were happy to receive the box and its contents. Bart recalled that Eric had worked at the building before he went into the service and also said that Eric suffered some type of amnesia from the war. Ruth and Amanda were very proud that they found the box, medals and watch so that the grandchildren would always have memories of their grandparents, Eric and Jan.

Ruth and Amanda both promised on their honor that they would never go on such adventures again so they told their mothers, Anita and Rosalie (of course this was not by actual count the 345th time they had promised the same thing) but since everything worked out well (strangely enough all or at least it seemed all of the adventures of Amanda and Ruth turned out well)

CHAPTER TWELVE - GROUND HOLE

Anita and Rosalie ended up as they usually did giving both Ruth and Amanda big hugs and saying how proud they were that the cousins seemed to find the right thing to do in their adventures.

CHAPTER THIRTEEN – MOTHERS' BIRTHDAYS

"What are we going to get our mothers this time?" Amanda asked Ruth. Ruth replied that they each had available $100.00 from their allowance. Ruth also said that their mothers, Anita and Rosalie were born on the same day one year apart. The mothers celebrated their birthdays on the same day each year.

Amanda and Ruth discussed possible presents ruling out clothes as being too expensive and in Ruth's words, redundant; jewelry was discarded on the basis that both mothers already had too much jewelry; perfume or bath soap or lotions was left as an option; handbags-belts were not given much consideration; special stationary would be acceptable.

Ruth suggested that she and Amanda should do what they enjoyed the most that is shop till they drop without buying anything unless they or one of them saw something to buy. They called Max and soon were at Macy's downtown store. Since the birthdays were a week sway they decided to forego visiting the children's clothing area and willingly avoided the toy department.

Amanda and Ruth despite their discussions, did spend a great deal of time perusing the clothing, perfume handbags, jewelry department fantasizing about buying several items well knowing these were not appropriate and way too expensive. Inspiration occurred and both Ruth and Amanda both thought of a good gift well within their available funds being Brazilian multi-colored scarves for $60.00 each. Ruth selected for her mother Anita, one with a rainbow hued and a golden border and splashes of pink, yellow and turquoise in the rainbow background. Amanda picked out for her mother, Rosalie, a scarf with bright blue and then several shades of blue interlacing

CHAPTER THIRTEEN - MOTHERS' BIRTHDAYS

this scarf with a faint red tinged heart placed off center. Ruth then thought of the idea of putting a metal holder on the end of each scarf with a suitable embossed saying thereon.

Each of them thought about what to say in ten words and spent about twenty minutes writing down their thoughts. Mundane and trite statements were considered and rejected including "love forever" and "you are the best mother" and similar cardboard routine sentiments.

Ruth wrote the following for Anita, her mother. . "Believe Dad will come home. Never give up".

Amanda thought of the inscription for her mother, Rosalie. "Light the candles of your spirit to achieve happiness."

They spent some time picking out boxes and wrapping both scarves and the inscribed scarf holders and presented them on silver trays to their mothers after enjoying a family birthday dinner for just the four of them and since the dinner was catered no one had to do any cooking or cleaning up afterward. Each of them, Anita, Rosalie, Ruth and Amanda selected their individual preferences so they all had exactly what they individually liked to eat and drink. There was a large oval cake, with a layer of white, a layer of chocolate, and a third multi-layer of raspberry and lemon, all covered with light and dark chocolate frosting. After they finished their meal and sang happy birthday and ate their slices of cake, arrangements were made to send a large piece of the cake down to Max since he had made sure all the food was delivered fresh hot and timely.

Then Anita and Rosalie opened their presents from their daughters and became emotional and somewhat overwhelmed at the

CHAPTER THIRTEEN - MOTHERS' BIRTHDAYS

thoughtfulness of both Ruth and Amanda not only in selecting useful and beautiful scarves as gifts but had difficulty believing that each of them had composed such meaningful inscriptions which were insightful and inspirational to each of them. A full round of hugs and kisses occurred and they all said that without question this was by far the best birthday they had ever had.

CHAPTER FOURTEEN - MEALS MENU

Amanda had a desk top computer and she and Ruth used it to learn and discover information on the internet although both preferred to read books for knowledge. They liked the fact that they could type documents and then print out and save them via the computer.

Ruth told Amanda "why don't we prepare a menu for drinking and eating and then print it out for our mothers, the nanny Rita and our part-time chef Kristy." Amanda thought this was great idea and thought it best to divide up the work. Ruth would do the breakfast and snacks menu and Amanda would do the lunch and dinner menu. It was also determined that Ruth since she had the sweeter tooth of both of them would devise the dessert treats.

Ruth's breakfast menu consisted of: Cereal-whole grain including cream of wheat or oatmeal or many processed cereals with fiber; Fruits including bananas, apples, oranges, grapes, cantaloupes and melons; Dairy products, whole vitamin D milk; Eggs which consisted of scrambled, poached, fried such as sunny-side up, soft-boiled but not hard boiled nor fancy omelets; Toast-raisin and cinnamon, and rye or whole wheat; Waffles and pancakes with honey or syrup.

Ruth showed this menu for breakfast to Amanda and they both became hungry so they printed out multiple copies so that Anita, Rosalie and the nanny Rita and their part-time chef/cook Kristy would have the menu for breakfast meals.

In preparing the breakfast menu, Amanda came up with the concept of printing all of their names on it and setting up blocks which could be checked to establish their individual choices and a special area was created so that each could add

CHAPTER FOURTEEN - MEALS MENU

additional selections so that the breakfast menu was personalized. There was a plan to keep information on the computer to establish what each one had as regular or favorite breakfast items but it was decided to leave that project for later.

Amanda started to work on the luncheon menu and proposed that the lunch would consist of lighter and more easily assembled items so that there would be little cooking roasting or baking required. Amanda's luncheon menu was store or bakery bought bagels or fresh bread; salad with many variations such as lettuce, radishes, carrots, spinach, kale, cauliflower, asparagus, with relishes and cheeses (for those inclined to actually eat cheese products); with the salads set up in covered containers so each could do their own preparation; lunch meats consisting of ham, chicken, turkey, sandwich pepperoni and the mystery maybe meat or not; fresh fruit of all kinds; hot canned soup-tomato-chicken broth or noodle, chowder, onion, celery, and several others; a tray of mixed nuts-almonds-cashews -peanuts-walnuts-pecans, etc.; obviously a relish tray of fresh celery, radish, and carrots; and for those who want this all varieties of fresh berries in season with real cream or ice cream. There was a printed disclaimer on this printed lunch menu that there would be no listing of calories nor any statements regarding obesity or health concerns. There was a statement that eating is always at the eater's own risk and subject to free will and choice.

Ruth came up with a snacks menu that was somewhat redundant since it contained most of the fresh fruit, nuts, and fresh vegetables but also had popcorn, buttered or not-salted or not;

CHAPTER FOURTEEN - MEALS MENU

favorite), chocolate covered raisins, peanuts and nuts; trail mix; puddings; jello, custards; and pies. On the printed menu, there was a message that these snacks should not be substitutes for eating a well-balanced (whatever that means) nutritionally appropriate diet in order to avoid all the eating disorders that could ensue.

Ruth came up with a serious dinner menu-pizza in infinite varieties; steak dinners with potatoes and gravy; canned corn and corn on the cob, peas, asparagus, tomatoes and fresh vegetables,; spaghetti and meatballs; Ham dinner-roast beef-pork chops (no lamb or veal meals set forth) chicken (cooked roasted baked or bought) and turkey with or without stuffing; all manner of fresh fruits and vegetables and even for the fast food addicts frozen repasts including meat balls and chicken fries.

Ruth had no problem in devising a dessert menu since she had the taste for sweets par excellence and she came up with (a caveat that there would be endless additions to this dessert menu since it was a truly a work in progress) ice cream by the scoop-the dish-the cup-by the quart or pint or half gallon/ gallon/multi-gallon or pies-cakes-muffins-cookies-doughnuts-candies made or store bought bakery dessert treats-grocery available treats-popsicles-puddings-custards-jello-chocolate milk found for these including fruit drinks and sodas. This menu when printed had seven double spaced detailed entries. Ruth later explained that she finally quit listing all of the desserts since she had mentally calculated that if she ate one of the dessert menu items per day that she would be 9 years and two months and six days old when she was at the end and that in

CHAPTER FOURTEEN - MEALS MENU

dessert items would be created produced or tasted.

Thus, Ruth and Amanda completed their menu computer printed project successfully.

CHAPTER FIFTEEN - WHY NO SEAFOOD

After the elaborate menus were prepared by Amanda and Ruth and printed out, Rosalie knew there was something drastically wrong and finally realized what it was when she went into one of the bathrooms and saw the toy whale. Rosalie exclaimed to Anita the nanny, the chef, and to Ruth and Amanda, "Where o' where is the seafood to select, cook, or not eat, savor and enjoy?" Both girls were mortified and repeatedly said they were sorry. Rosalie told all assembled that she would prepare the seafood menu and she did as follows:

The Forgotten Seafood Menu

(To be meticulously selected-—prepared by cooking—-boiling—frying-—roasting—-toasting--deep fried—-fresh or raw—-to suit everyone's or anyone's taste or appetite)

Oysters — half or full shell or nude

Crabs - good or if desired crabby disposition

Lobster - large or tiny - boiled but not raw

Sushi - to be an acquired taste

Shrimp - mostly large—in or out of shell—cooked—steamed—boiled-deep fried-covered with anything desired including strawberries, hot or cold chocolate, nuts of exquisite variety, coconut, garlic, roots of sassafras, or any concoction or confection imaginable.

Fish-in unbelievable quantities but always of superb quality-prepared with wine or liqueur always tasteful and filling.

Free Dessert from Dessert menu

CHAPTER SIXTEEN – USE FEET/NO HANDS

Amanda and Ruth were at the Public Library in late March when they saw an announcement stating that all children who are five years old can play soccer on an all boys team; an all girls team; or on a coed team with practices after sign up starting May 1st and games to be played in June and July. Soccer shoes and shin guards are mandatory and only five year olds who have not previously played soccer can sign up. Experienced soccer players are encouraged to join regular soccer league.

Ruth and Amanda thought this would be a good idea and discussed this with Max on the cab ride home and Max, who was loyal, strong and protective, said he would practice with them since he knew a lot about soccer. He said if their mothers agreed he would help them pick out soccer shoes and shin guards, telling them to select boys' soccer shoes since those shoes were studier and fit feet better. He asked them what is the essential soccer rule and Ruth said to run fast and swerve and Amanda said to make goals and win. Max responded that the cardinal rule of soccer is "Use Feet/No Hands"—and kept repeating that the only use of hands is for the goalie and when players are throwing the soccer ball back into play.

Back at the apartment, Amanda and Ruth showed the soccer application to Anita and Rosalie and since Max was present, his advice to sign up for the co-ed team was accepted after he told all of them that the boys may be stronger and perhaps faster but that by the girls playing with and against boys that all would acquire more self-confidence and play and enjoy the game far more.

The advice of Max was accepted and the application forms for both Amanda and Ruth were sent in with the appropriate fees.

CHAPTER SIXTEEN - USE FEET/NO HANDS

Max was asked to take the girls to the sport store which they used and Max said he would do so if he had the final word on what to buy. The store had an extensive soccer department and although both girls did not like the color selections of the boys' soccer shoes they listened to Max and bought the best fitting sturdy soccer shores. Amanda and Ruth convinced Max so they could buy colorful designed shin guards and they purchased matching pink, yellow and dark blue small size shin guards. They tried on these shoes of guards before leaving the store and they also bought two properly sized soccer balls again heeding the advice of Max so they did not buy the most costly soccer balls but bought the second least expensive ones on the basis of their durability.

Max set up a practice schedule for the last three weeks of April before team practices would commence on May first and they went to the practice field with Max four times a week even when it was raining and the soccer field was both wet and muddy and slippery. At the first practice both   Amanda and Ruth constantly violated the paramount soccer rule not to touch, catch or use their hands whatsoever. Max repeated this rule so often that both girls started mimicking Max in sing song fashion. Max stayed silent but at the next practice provided both of them with sleeveless sweaters and had them take off their other sweaters and pull on the new sweaters which kept their arms and hands inside so that it was impossible to even come close to touching the soccer ball with their hands. At first they both had trouble running after the ball since their balance was interfered with by the non-use of hands and they could not extend their arms to maintain balance. However, both of them, with Amanda having the greater stamina and Ruth being

CHAPTER SIXTEEN - USE FEET/NO HANDS

the speedier started to master the art and skill of moving the soccer ball by nudging, kicking and pushing only with their feet the soccer balls.

During the final week of April, max showed and taught Ruth and Amanda some soccer truths and tricks to use the inside of the foot, both right and left, to kick the ball rather than the shoe toe explaining there would be both more distance and far better control using the inside portion of shoes. Max also demonstrated using the outside of the shoe to create a diversion and unexpected soccer shot and said this might help to avoid the goalie who could use body, head, feet, arms, and hands to catch or deflect the ball. Max further showed them how to control and dribble the ball with their feet only.

By the end of April they were ready for soccer practice and playing—"Use Feet/No Hands".

CHAPTER SEVENTEEN – RUTH'S LOST BOX

Ruth, sometime after living with Amanda, realized one morning that she did not have a box that she had helped her mother, Anita, pack which contained her third and four year memories and she struggled to remember what was in the box. Ruth recalled a photograph album and this had pictures of herself, her third birthday party, her swimming attempts but far more importantly a series of photos of her dad and since he vanished when Ruth was two months past her third birthday there would be no other photos. Packed in the box so Ruth recalled were some of her toys and a collection of McDonald's Happy Meal toys amounting to almost 56 toys although she could not be more exact. Ruth believed there were birthday, holiday and Christmas cards and a few letters not including the last one her dad had written when he left.

Ruth did remember that she had used a Sunday newspaper comic section to wrap around the box and put colorful green and orange ribbons to tie the box and used silver colored duct tape to secure the box and its contents.

Ruth hurried to the kitchen and asked Anita where her three and four year old memory box was. Anita immediately took Ruth with Amanda following to the basement storage area where there were many boxes and unused furniture items and where Ruth and Amanda found their toy automobiles, being a yellow corvette for Amanda and a tan Jeep for Ruth and both girls started up the vehicles which despite the length of time they had sat idle still ran. Anita directed them to the stored boxes and the thereof them moved all of the boxes but could not locate the special box that Ruth had wrapped. They spent over an hour in the large storage area with no success.

CHAPTER SEVENTEEN - RUTH'S LOST BOX

Upon returning to the apartment, Anita found the moving company papers and called the office. The situation was explained and the movers called back a little later and said there were two shipments and this specific box was listed on the second shipment along with a dresser and three other boxes. Anita said that none of these items were delivered and insisted on the movers researching this promptly. Early the next morning the moving company said they had the missing items located in another storage facility in Atlanta, Georgia and could not understand nor explain how this happened. At any rate they said they would ship the items at once and they should arrive in a week. Ruth marked up her calendar so she could make certain when her memory box would come.

It took a week and two days but the delivery truck did arrive and the items were delivered and each of the new found items were inspected and inventoried.

Ruth with the help of Amanda carried the decorated box to Ruth's bedroom where using shears and brute strength they succeeded in removing all of the wrapping materials and Ruth lovingly took each precious memory from the box with the very first thing she looked at was a thick envelope addressed to my Little R. in her dad's handwriting. He had vanished and not heard from so this was the next to last word Ruth had from him except his last brief letter. While Ruth was carefully removing the letters from the envelope, Amanda observing that this was quite emotional for Ruth and told Ruth she would leave her alone for awhile and would look at the photo album and Ruth's toys later.

CHAPTER SEVENTEEN - RUTH'S LOST BOX

Ruth took her time unfolding the older letters from her dad and since his handwriting was bold and legible started to read those three.

Ruth after reading the three letters placed them back in the envelope and cried.

Ruth called out for Amanda to come back in so they could look through the photo album which they did being amused at how young Ruth looked and had different hairstyles and such dorky clothes. They spent well over an hour together with Amanda quite often hugging Ruth causing Ruth to feel much better. They spent a little time examining the toys with both of them wondering what they ever saw in such babyish toys since Amanda said she had duplicates of just about all the toys that Ruth had except that Ruth actually had a red slinky toy whereas Amanda said she had a blue one. A few dolls were different. Amanda did express her admiration for the Happy Meal toy collection and they decided to put them on one of the shelves in Ruth's bedroom

Anita was asked to take a picture of Ruth and Amanda with outstretched arms pointing at the collection and three photos were taken. That morning Ruth also placed a photograph of her dad next to one of her mother and put the recent picture of herself and Amanda in the middle.

CHAPTER EIGHTEEN – SOCCER MIXED WITH MUD

The soccer team that Amanda and Ruth played on was a mixture of eight girls and four boys, all age 5 and with zero experience. They played a twelve game schedule in June and July. They had teal-colored shirts with a light red circle colored in on which the HANDS was across the circle in bright blue with a black diagonal line through the word HANDS so that their name was "Hands Not".

The team had won one game, lost one game and tied two games up to the day they were facing an unbeaten and untied team called the Victors and this team although with different players had been unbeaten with no ties for the past two soccer seasons.

When they arrived, there was a sign stating that the game could not be played at the regular field but had to be played at a somewhat bumpy field and since it had rained this field was wet and a little muddy. Ruth volunteered to be goalie for the first half and although Amanda had not been goalie before she agreed to be the second half goalie. They played six on a side and this day four of their players were not present but in contrast the other team had all twelve available. The league provided as a rule that every player must play at least one-half of each game. All immediately noticed a boy on the other team who was over six inches taller than the others and was large and mean looking and had a reputation from other players on other teams to be aggressive. It started to rain and a few minutes before the game was to start there was a severe downpour but no thunder or lightning. The league had a rule that games would be played even if raining so long as there was no danger to the players. The field became even muddier than it had been but the rain was light and there was a wind of about 10 miles per hour.

CHAPTER EIGHTEEN - SOCCER MIXED WITH MUD

The players ran slower because the grass was slippery and they found that the soccer ball ended up in the muddiest of areas. Ruth batted the ball away from the goal area with her doubled up fists and on three other occasions grabbed hold of the soccer ball smothering it with her body and prevented any scoring by the other team. The large boy on the other team could not run very fast and was removed and replaced on two occasions in the first half.

Ruth in putting the ball back in play used the side of her foot and kicked it as shown to her by Max and was able to kick the ball over the heads of some of the players and usually kicked it over 20 yards. Anita, Rosalie, and Max watched the game and took some photos. They had rain gear and umbrellas. There was no score by either team and a few parents said the game should end and the second half not played due to the rain and mud. Players on both teams insisted on completing the game and made remarks "Why don't you spectators who can't stand the rain so go sit in your cars" and "we are not sissies and can take the rain and mud". Without further ado, the two teams played the second half which involved heavier rain and more mud so that it was difficult to tell the colors of the shirts. The players subbing in sometimes had umbrellas but of course the players on the field did not. Amanda played goalie with verve and on at least two occasions prevented a goal by sliding face forward through a muddy area to deflect the ball. Despite valiant effort by several players no one could score a goal so that the game ended in a zero-zero tie, and there was no sudden death shootout permitted. Many pictures were taken of individual players and each of the teams so that there would be a fond memory of this outstanding soccer game. Both teams made

CHAPTER EIGHTEEN - SOCCER MIXED WITH MUD

it a point to state that they would be playing each other in four weeks and some remarked that they hoped it would rain again.

Max drove his cab with Amanda, Ruth, Rosalie and Anita to a New York restaurant and although Ruth and Amanda changed their soccer shoes and shin guards they insisted on keeping on their thoroughly muddied shirts. They did go into the bathroom and cleaned their hands, arms, legs, and faces and had their hair combed out before sitting down for the best treat they ordered, with Ruth having both a strawberry milkshake and a pineapple sundae and Amanda only having the extra large banana split with three scoops of ice cream. They both had to eat a ham sandwich and a small glass of milk before they could enjoy the dessert.

CHAPTER NINETEEN – CRAZY SOCCER SEASON

By all accounts the first soccer season was very unusual even by the standards of Amanda and Ruth since crazy things happened.

The first one occurred when someone over inflated the soccer ball so that when Ruth kicked it with the side of her foot intending for the ball to go about ten yards to a teammate at her left side but instead the ball bounced high over the heads of two defending players then took several small bounces and just as the opposing goalie reached for it, the soccer ball bounced high over the arms of that goalie and caromed into the net so that Ruth scored her second goal of the season without having the slightest intention of doing so.

In the same game when Amanda was playing forward she kicked a different soccer ball and it was heading for the net and would score a goal based on the position of the goalie since she had tripped and was laying prone on the ground and in no position to reach the ball, when the ball which had been a little soft suddenly went flat and stopped its forward motion about an inch or two from giving Amanda her second goal. Another opposing player kicked the now flat ball away.

During the final game of the season, an opposing player turned around and kicked a great shot past his own goalie and it was such a perfectly executed kick that every one cheered although that goal won the game for the "Hands Not" team of Amanda and Ruth.

Earlier in the same final game, an opposing player threw the ball in to initiate a play and threw the ball so hard that

CHAPTER NINETEEN - CRAZY SOCCER SEASON

it bounced and skidded past the goalie and into the net, which created a tie game at that time.

In first half a player again on the opposing team kicked the soccer ball from midfield so well that it shot past the outstretched arms of the goalie and this resulted in a tremendous roar from the crowd.

The other unusual occurrence in this game was when a player on Amanda and Ruth's team who was the goalie at that time and who had been learning and practicing the side foot kick actually kicked the soccer ball so it flew bounced and skidded into the opposite goal amazing all of the players and spectators and the officials.

In comments made, no one who observed all of these remarkable events could ever recall any one game or for that matter any soccer season where such unusual or crazy kicks and damaged balls had ever happened.

There was a universal agreement by all those concerned that this had far exceeded any expectation of what a soccer game and season should be and they all said they looking forward to the next soccer season which would start on September first and last for two months. Amanda and Ruth mentioned there were indoor soccer leagues also.

CHAPTER TWENTY - SOCCER SWEATER

Both Amanda and Ruth noticed in a soccer practice that several of their teammates, particularly Audrey, a stocky red-haired girl, and Art, a shy thin boy, had real difficulty in not using their hands to control the ball. They asked Audrey and Art to wear their sleeveless sweaters and they agreed to do so. Audrey had immediate trouble keeping her feet and fell several times while having her arms pinned inside the sweater since she needed her arms for balance but Audrey was getting better at just kicking the ball so she kept this sleeveless sweater on. Art likewise had difficulty and tried on occasion to find ways to use his arms and hands but he also made the effort and found rewards when the coaches praised him for running and kicking the ball. Both Audrey and Art were encouraged to be the goalie so they could play soccer using their arms and hands but unfortunately Art was afraid of getting hit in the face by the soccer ball and Audrey had the habit if a ball was hit near her of turning sideways so that the ball passed by her and into the net. They both continued to practice with the sleeveless sweaters. Audrey, when taking the ball from outside the lines to throw it, simply rolled the sweater up to her neck and threw the ball into play and then swiftly pulled the sweater down so she could play just to kick the ball. Art started to complain that he had an itchy and snotty nose and needed his hands free to use his handkerchief to blow his nose so Art quit using the sweater for awhile. Then Art got into big trouble since he struck the ball twice with his hands and rather than being sidelined Art determined to become a good soccer player donned the sweater again.

The coach, Randy, asked the team if they wanted to not only practice using sleeveless sweaters but also whether they would like to play a game wearing such sweaters and they all agreed it was a good idea. At the next practice everyone had fitted sweaters and the coach showed off his goalie sweater which was a pullover with both sleeves cut off so that the player acting as goalie would have his or her arms completely free. The sweaters had their team name "Hand Not" there on along with their names.

The practice session went very well and the coach checked with the league officials and they said there was no rule against players wearing sleeveless sweaters. The team played the next league game using their special sweaters and they played so well that they won that game by the score of 4 to 2 and were very happy.

The coach then told all of them that they could practice in those sweaters but that they had to play the rest of the league games without using the sweaters on the basis that they should learn to play soccer in a normal and usual fashion. This was accepted without dissent since the players realized that they were now good soccer players and have learned to play with feet, bodies and heads, but no hands except for the goalie.

CHAPTER TWENTY ONE - RESCUE DOG

One morning in the summer, Amanda and Ruth were taken by Rosalie to visit the nearby fire station and they were introduced to the fire department personnel and had an educational time looking at and exploring the fire trucks, equipment and machinery. They were allowed to climb up on the huge fire truck with the large extension ladder. Each of them was shown the multiple controls and they were permitted to turn the large steering wheel. Ruth was placed inside a suit that fire fighters use to go into a fire and in putting the mask on felt lost and somewhat frightened. Both were asked to lift the hose head of the fire hose and could barely lift it above the cement where it was placed.

Amanda asked and was granted permission to use her cell phone camera to take pictures and she took pictures of the large fire hall, the various trucks and close-ups of the equipment and each of the firemen there. She said she would eventually create a photo album labeled "Trip to the fire hall" with a date and clearly marked captions—she thought of creating a video of the visit but decided that the photo album was a sufficient memory.

When they were on that visit, Ruth noticed a small dog and was told that it was a stray and sometimes came to the fire hall and ran around making short yelps and when the fire truck went out, the dog often ran after it barking and on two occasions stopped and let out a continuous howl, with a fireman, Mike, remarking that on those two occasions there was a serious fire and in both fires a person was injured by the fire and was hospitalized but did survive. On all other runs the dog barked but did not yowl. Ruth wanted to name the dog "danger" and

CHAPTER TWENTY ONE - RESCUE DOG

Amanda thought of "warning". They discussed this and compromised by calling the little dog "Asher". Strangely enough, each time Amanda or Ruth called out the name Asher, the dog did not respond.

A week or so later after their fire hall visit, Amanda and Ruth started to hear unusual sounds which seemed to come from the inner wall of Ruth's closet. It was faint and became louder when Ruth and/or Amanda pressed her ear to the wall. It sounded like a yip with a pause and another yip. Ruth had been studying the Morse code and believed that this was a code for help but it was not clear enough to establish that.

Amanda and Ruth put on their backpacks so they would have gloves, a first aid kit and flashlights along with their digital phone cameras.

They decided not to take the elevator since they had previously explored the building so they knew where the stairs were located to access the roof and they quietly made their way to the rooftop believing that the sound came from there. They had a roll of duct tape and scissors so they carefully placed duct tape over the lock mechanism so that the door did not shut and be locked. They walked out on the roof and walked around the perimeter and looked down onto the street-a long way down. Ruth remarked to Amanda about how tiny people and cars and even a bus looked and Amanda said what about coming here on Halloween and tossing water balloons off the roof. Ruth told Amanda they should be quiet and listen for the yip sounds since she was certain that it was in trouble and needed help.

CHAPTER TWENTY ONE – RESCUE DOG

Amanda and Ruth listened and finally heard yips coming from a vent for air conditioning. They shone the flashlights and saw a tiny dog wedged in the vent. Ruth hung a Twix candy bar on a string and lowered it down to the dog but the dog would not bite and turned its head away. Amanda said maybe we should try a Hershey bar instead but Ruth remarked maybe the dog was scared and did not want to eat candy. Ruth stayed there while Amanda went to get Anita and tell her what they found. Anita promptly called the fire department and they came and after some effort freed the dog. Ruth and Amanda both exclaimed with one voice "Why that dog is "Asher" but the dog refused to listen to that name and instead hid behind Anita. Anita wisely took he dog accompanied by Ruth and Amanda to the closest dog shelter where it was discovered that the dog had been missing for some time and was really named Jerry and was soon reunited with its owners.

CHAPTER TWENTY TWO - BETRAYAL

Alice was envious of Rosalie and Anita because they each had clever daughters and Alice had a son who was an imp and who caused trouble whenever he was out in public. Alice decided to lose a bracelet and then claim that the nanny Rita at Rosalie's apartment stole it.

There was a book club meeting and Alice was invited since she had been an editor at a publishing house for some years until she left for unexplained reasons and Rosalie felt that Alice would lend some new flair to the book discussions.

Alice went to a jewelry store and had a replica made of her bracelet made and started to wear the fake one and kept the original in her wall safe. She started to make comments about how precious and valuable the bracelet was and how it was a gift to her from her aunt, Sara, who had appeared on Broadway both in a drama and in a musical. Then Alice made appoint of saying she never wanted the bracelet to be stolen and she was insuring it for an increased amount.

Alice came to the book club meeting and she had made sure that the bracelet could be easily detached. She waited till no attention was being paid to her and she removed the bracelet and placed it in the jacket that she had observed hanging in the entry way which she knew was Rita's jacket since Rita had just brought Amanda and Ruth home. Alice carefully closed the pocket tightly so the bracelet would remain there. A little later, Alice asked Rosalie if Rita could go the lobby and see if there was available a tour map of Central Park since she wanted to use the guide to make informed remarks relating to the book being discussed. Rita was called in and Alice talked to her explaining what she needed and made sure that Rita was observed

CHAPTER TWENTY TWO - BETRAYAL

in close proximity to Alice. Alice reminded Rita to take her jacket with her.

A few minutes after Rita left, Alice exclaimed that her precious bracelet was missing. Everyone started to look for the bracelet but to no avail. Alice started to cry and then said to everyone that when Rita was close to her she did feel funny but thought nothing of it. Rita returned and gave the guide map to Alice and Alice asked Rita whether she took the bracelet and Rita responded "no". Rita then said to search her and the bracelet was found in the closed pocket of her jacket. Amanda and Ruth came into the room having heard the uproar and defended Rita. Ruth looked in the pocket and found a small wad of paper which when opened was a receipt for a bracelet from the jewelry shop and it turned out that Alice had wrapped the bracelet with the receipt without realizing that she had done so. Needless to say Alice was dismissed with extreme prejudice from the book club and Rita was invited to take her place which she did and helped to make this book blub enviable and her first selection was the "story of the purloined necklace".

CHAPTER TWENTY THREE - PEANUT BUTTER FIGHT

Many people thought that Amanda and Ruth were sisters, not in looks but because they were together so much and seemed to do the same activities but in fact, they had many dislikes and the most serious was peanut butter.

Amanda loved peanut butter and simply adored the smoothness of it and overtly enjoyed the aroma but most of all simply loved the taste of peanut butter. She spread it on toast and bagels and on celery and bananas and she especially used peanut butter to enhance ice cream, regardless of the flavor of the ice cream. If Amanda had a sundae, say a strawberry flavored one, she would, if at home, take out the jar of peanut butter no matter what brand and put at leas two heaping tablespoons of peanut butter on her sundae. Amanda had the annoying habit of making moaning sighs while eating or licking peanut butter. She would take the peanut butter container when it was almost empty and using a knife and a spoon would make certain she removed every trace of the peanut butter of course, eating or swallowing it so that the container was as empty as possible before discarding it in the trash compactor.

Amanda will always remember her fourth birthday when her mother Rosalie, and her aunt, Anita, brought her large containers of peanut butter so that Amanda would for sure have a sufficient supply.

ON the other hand, Ruth abhorred peanut butter and could not even stand for a container even if unopened to be in her presence. Ruth always said once she tasted peanut butter and she became ill but when Ruth was tested for an allergic reaction to peanut butter she showed zero problem although she claimed to have thrown up immediately after being exposed by way of the

CHAPTER TWENTY THREE - PEANUT BUTTER FIGHT

allergy test to a miniscule amount of peanut butter. Ruth would not only make caustic remarks when Amanda or anyone else was eating peanut butter in her presence but tried on many occasions to leave the table and await till the peanut butter eating was completed.

One time, Ruth claimed that Amanda played a dirty trick by putting peanut butter in a cupcake by using a syringe and Ruth said she knew this because of the color and smoothness of the small amount of cupcake filling. Anita on that occasion tasted part of the cupcake and said the filling was chocolate mousse and neither tasted like or smelled like peanut butter but Ruth would not eat any of the cupcakes. Ruth went to the trouble of reciting a ditty —"Peanut butter is for peanut brains and it is a scientific fact that those who eat this horrid mixture will lose their hearing", directed at Amanda every time Amanda was eating peanut butter but Amanda responded by stating that those "who ate peanut butter were better soccer players".

Ruth loved black olives and Amanda adored green olives and neither like the other kind so they got to share and have a monopoly of olives when olives were available. Amanda to make peace gave Ruth a supply of black olives and provided them in a sterile peanut butter jar and Ruth laughed.

CHAPTER TWENTY FOUR - TOYS OF THEIR FATHERS

At a time when Amanda and Ruth were in the living room with their mothers, Rosalie and Anita, Ruth asked a question, "What toys did our dads play with when they were little boys?" Rosalie answered that Ted, Amanda's dad, had played with model planes, sometimes with and sometimes without mothers and that Ted enjoyed building the models. Anita told Ruth that Richard, her dad, had a favorite toy he constantly played with being an erector set. They all went to the basement storage area and a non-motorized erector set was located along with a model airplane kit which was still in its original box.

They all went to the toy and craft room which was also the den and Amanda and Rosalie carefully opened the box containing the spitfire model airplane and started to read the detailed instructions. They then laid out the various parts to make sure that all needed parts were available and only then did Amanda with the help of Rosalie commence to relive the past of her dad, Ted, had accomplished so often when he was perhaps seven years old. Rosalie located an Xacto knife set and found glue so paper could be placed to cover the airplane frame as Amanda constructed it. There was insignia to be put on the plane. They worked on constructing the spitfire plane for several days and Amanda and Rosalie enjoyed the time together. Amanda woke up each morning with the expectation that she would be in some sense walking in her dead father's footsteps and he was guiding her in building and designing the spitfire airplane. When it was finished, at the suggestion of Rosalie it was called Ted and was proudly displayed on the living room mantel next to a photograph (the last one) of Ted, Rosalie and Amanda.

CHAPTER TWENTY FOUR - TOYS OF THEIR FATHERS

At the same time the model plane was started, Ruth asked her mother, Anita, to help her to read and understand the erector set instructions and to aid her in building something that her father Richard would have enjoyed building. Initially, Anita was reluctant to do this project but soon put aside her feelings and decided to bond with and help Ruth since this specific erector set was geared to age ten plus. The instructions although in English, appeared to be written by engineers (and they were) and Anita had to resort to a dictionary in order to understand the complicated and convoluted instructions. Anita told Ruth that probably a college scientific education was necessary to fully understand the instructions. With some anxiety they decided to build an elevator and they laid out the nuts, bolts, steel beams of various sizes. The gears, wheels, pulleys, axles, and other pars they had difficulty naming. Anita, being a perfectionist at heart, made sure that all needed parts to build the elevator and to insure that once built it would be operable were on the craft table. Ruth, with the absolutely necessary help of Anita spent four days being constantly frustrated at the intricate use of small tools and making sure all the metal parts stayed together an supported the next part. Many a time, Anita expressed the wish that Richard had used Lincoln logs or Legos or some other vastly simpler toy than the infuriating Erector set. Ruth and Anita stayed faithful to the task they set themselves and did achieve the building of a working elevator. They were proud of this venture and they used the working elevator to raise and lower items such as small toys and jewelry. The finished elevator was also displayed on the other

CHAPTER TWENTY FOUR - TOYS OF THEIR FATHERS

side of the mantel with a card stating "made by Ruth and Anita." "Inspired by the memory of Richard."

CHAPTER TWENTY FIVE - FARM TRIP

The school that Amanda and Ruth attended arranged to visit
a working farm which had chickens, goats, sheep, horses and
cows. There was a large barn and a sizeable chicken coop to
hold 80 chickens of various breeds. Many schools had outings at
this farm and it was a well-organized visit. There was an
enclosed are similar to a petting zoo where baby or young
animals were housed. There were 14 students including Amanda
and Ruth. Amanda had a special interest in lambs, whereas Ruth
favored baby chicks. They had their photo cameras with them and
after they arrived they started to take pictures of the
surroundings, the farm buildings, the farm equipment and took
numerous photos of the animals and some far away shots in the
fields and enclosures. Before entering the petting area, both
Amanda and Ruth took pictures of the animals there including
many of their school class mates.

Amanda and Rut enjoyed being amidst the animals and picked
some up and petted them. As typical for them, they walked away,
and entered the barn and soon were climbing on the tractor, the
combine, the manure spreader, the harvester and played on them
as though they were actually operating such machines. They were
discovered and decided to join their class mates in the corn
maze which proved to be quite challenging since Ruth succeeded
in getting lost in this maze, thereby triggering a concentrated
search. Ruth crawled through a small opening and proceeded to
crawl due north until she found her way out. She then walked to
the maze entrance asking others what was happening. Everyone
was so happy that Ruth was no longer lost that they did not
blame Ruth for frightening them. Amanda succeeded in
antagonizing the two large geese so that she was chased around
the yard by such geese till she found some balls and using her

soccer kicking skills kicked the balls striking the geese in their chest area causing the geese to quit chasing her.

Amanda was inclined to take one of the lambs home but was dissuaded by Ruth because they had no lamb food so she suggested instead that Ruth should put one of the chicks in her backpack. Ruth refused on the logical basis that the chick would be hungry and might suffocate. They almost had a serious argument but made up realizing that some of their ideas were foolish.

On arriving home, Amanda and Ruth showed the pictures to all present and had several printed out to be placed in their school photo album. They regaled their mothers with their varied exploits and said they had a very informative and enjoyable visit to the farm.

CHAPTER TWENTY SIX - ELEVATOR

Ruth and Amanda were talking one evening before bedtime and Ruth said "School starts in three days and we should have one last adventure." Amanda agreed and suggested that they should visit the condemned building down the street before it is demolished. They recalled getting in twice before but had little time there. Ruth stated "Remember the old elevator we discovered but did not find out if it still ran? Amanda responded that it was their next adventure.

The next morning Ruth told Max and their mothers, Anita and Rosalie, that she and Amanda would spend the morning in the neighborhood.

Right after breakfast, they walked about a block away and easily found the hole they used before and the loose boards that had been placed over a door and entered the building.

They each had their adventure kit—two flashlights –needed food and drink—cell phones--- warm clothes and sturdy shoes and many other items. They always had with them pens and paper, cans of pepper spray and for sure those girl items needed including their special makeup kit.

So prepared, they went to the musty elevator and found that it opened easily. The elevator was quite roomy and could with ease hold twenty adults.

The elevator had buttons for floors one through six and two others, one for the basement and one for the sub-basement.

They spent an enjoyable hour or more stopping at most of the floors exploring. Ruth had a small efficient recorder and spoke into it recording her impression of the elevator, the

CHAPTER TWENTY SIX - ELEVATOR

building that they explored but found little new or memorable. The last floor was the third one and they stopped there. This third floor contained boxes and items stored throughout. Ruth used her handy scout knife and opened a few boxes. The boxes contained Christmas ornaments and toys from several decades ago. Both Amanda and Ruth very carefully handled and admired these antiques. After an hour Amanda suggested they should go home and tell the others about their adventure and discoveries.

They returned to the elevator and the door closed. The light suddenly went out. They retrieved their flashlights and found to their dismay that the elevator wouldn't move no matter what they tried. Ruth tried her cell phone and it registered "no service". Amanda's cell phone did likewise, Ruth had been reading about electricity and she opened the electric panel and told Amanda that there was no power.

Large noises started to vibrate within the elevator and soon both Amanda and Ruth realized this was the day the building would be demolished. Neither had seen on entering the building any warning signs but since they entered by a side boarded up door that omission was easily explained.

Amanda said, "We are trapped in the elevator which will not move. No one knows we are here. We are together on what may be our last adventure and there is no one I would rather be with." Ruth concurred. They calmly waited for what was to be talking to each other and then eating and drinking the food and drink they had.

In the meanwhile, Rosalie and Anita with Max and Dave had gathered in the living room and all were worried.

CHAPTER TWENTY SIX - ELEVATOR

Max, the last to arrive, pulled out his IPad and pushed some buttons. Max said "I know where they both are since I had a GPS app installed in both of their cell phones and also in their "adventure kits". As you know their cell phones are not operating". They piled into Max's cab and drove to the GPS blinking yellow light location. There was a demolition company commencing work.

Dave knew this company and located the supervisor and told him two young girls were in the building. This was confirmed when a workman told the boss about the door that was no longer boarded up.

The front door was pried open and Max led the way followed by Anita and Rosalie. Dave followed. The GPS device was the state-of-the-art and soon located Amanda and Ruth in the trapped elevator on the third floor. The supervisor tried to re-install electricity so the secure locked elevator door could open but was not successful.

Dave said "provide me with these tools and I can open this door." Rosalie located the hidden master receptacle where the electronics controlling the elevator was. Anita knew about the inner workings and went to work seeking to bypass the non-functioning electrical problem. Max used another device to communicate through the elevator door with the girls. Dave succeeded in forcing the elevator door open.

Amanda and Ruth had taken only a few bites of their sandwiches and sipped from their drink when the rescue occurred.

They gave a cursory rapid statement about their adventure. They then told the supervisor, Ronald, about all the antique

CHAPTER TWENTY SIX - ELEVATOR

treasures they had found. Ronald made several calls and shut down the building demolition till the antiques could be removed and either put in a museum or returned to the owners.

Ruth and Amanda were not scolded but praised for preserving this vast treasure of antiques which otherwise would have been destroyed forever.

However, Rosalie, Anita, Max, and Dave required Amanda and Ruth to never again embark on an adventure without communicating where they would be "adventuring".

In all their future adventures and there were many, Amanda and Ruth kept that pledge.

CHAPTER TWENTY SEVEN - HAPPINESS

Everything was relatively peaceful in the apartment complex. Amanda and Ruth were not planning any further adventures for the moment. They are preparing to attend public school in two days and will be together in first grade even though they are not yet six years old.

Ted is still remembered by all including Max and Dave with the two-year anniversary of his death occurring three weeks ago.

Ruth and Anita and the others have not forgotten that Richard has not been heard of for in excess of two years. The matra of Anita and Ruth is still strong and resolute that Richard will come home.

There was early in the day an occasion whereby Rosalie, Anita, Amanda, Ruth, Max and Dave enjoyed brunch. Dave told Amanda they would walk for a little while and when they reached the nearby park he had something important to talk to Amanda about. Amanda held hands with Dave while they silently walked. Amanda spent the time thinking about her dad and the reality of the very good relationship between her mom and Dave.

They sat together on a park bench. Dave opened the conversation by asking Amanda about her feelings about Dave's rapport with Rosalie and herself.

Without hesitating, Amanda told Dave that she loved him and wanted him to be always in the lives of herself and her mom.

Amanda followed up and directly asked Dave when he was going to propose to Rosalie. Dave said, "When we get back home. I wanted to talk to you first and in effect gain your approval and consent to this marriage. I wanted to be sure that your

CHAPTER TWENTY SEVEN – HAPPINESS

memory of your dad, Ted, would not prevent your acceptance of me."

Amanda said, "I hope you have a ring with you. Let us hurry home." They did not run back but did arrive home rapidly.

Without more ado, Dave at once asked Rosalie to marry him expressing his profound love for her and Amanda.

This proposal and the presenting of the Emerald engagement ring by Dave to Rosalie was met by sustained applause from Amanda, Ruth, Anita, and Max. Fittingly on the mantel of the living room there was the photograph of Ted and Richard together on display.

The rest of the afternoon was spent in enjoyable discussion and fond memories of Ted and Richard and recalling some of the adventures of Ruth and Amanda.

Anita had ordered a catered supper meal to be delivered around seven p.m.

A knock came on the door of the apartment and Ruth was asked to go to the door.

Ruth opened the door but it was not the catered supper delivery person in the doorway but a man stood there. Ruth cried out "Father, you have come home". Richard seized Ruth and gave her an intense hug. Richard entered and was at once in the fierce embrace of Anita.

Richard had come home forever and happiness reigned.